DO LIKE KYLA

A Richard Jackson Book

DO LIKE KYLA

by Angela Johnson

paintings by James E. Ransome

Orchard Books · New York

Orchard Books, 95 Madison Avenue, New York, NY 10016

Manufactured in the United States of America.
Book design by Mina Greenstein. The text of this book is set in 18 pt. ITC Esprit Medium.
The illustrations are oil paintings, reproduced in halftone.
Hardcover 10 9 8 7 6 5 4 3
Paperback 10 9 8 7 6 5 4 3 2

Library of Congress Cataloging-in-Publication Data
Johnson, Angela. Do like Kyla / by Angela Johnson ; illustrated by James E. Ransome.   p.   cm.
"A Richard Jackson book"—Cover. Summary: A little girl imitates her big sister Kyla all day, until in the evening Kyla imitates her. ISBN 0-531-05852-2.   ISBN 0-531-08452-3 (lib. bdg.)   [1. Sisters—Fiction.]   I. Ransome, James, ill.   II. Title.   PZ7.J629Do   1990   [E]—dc20   89-16229   CIP   AC

To my brothers, Keith and Kent

A.J.

To the two most important women in my life,
the late Mrs. Ruby G. Ransome and Lesa M. Cline

J.E.R.

In the morning my big sister Kyla stands at the window, tapping at the birds.
I do like Kyla, only standing on the bed.

Kyla pulls her sweater over her head and stretches.
I do like Kyla.

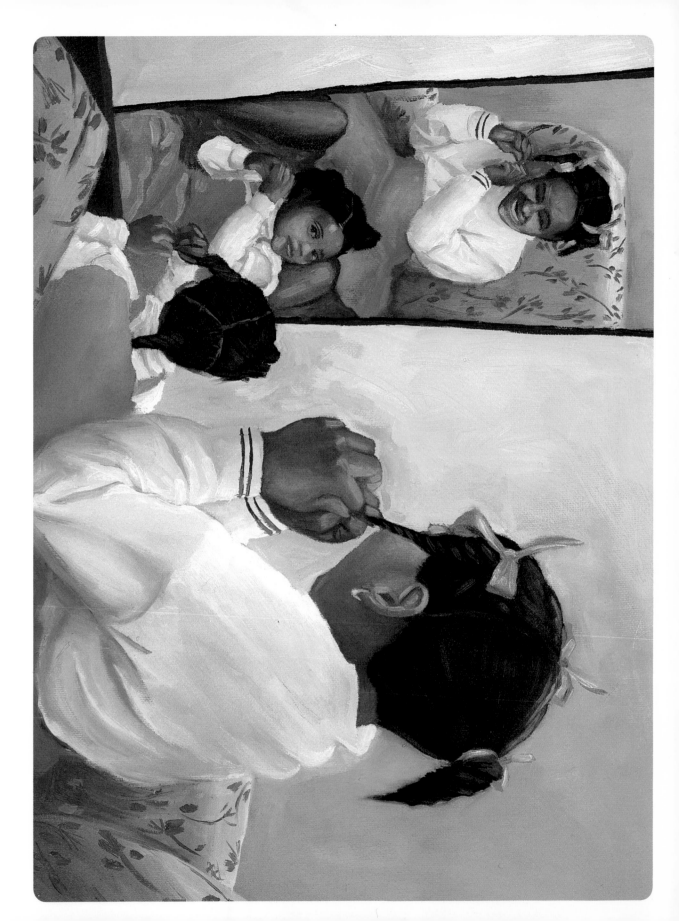

We sit in front of the big mirror in our room, and Kyla braids her hair with quick fingers.

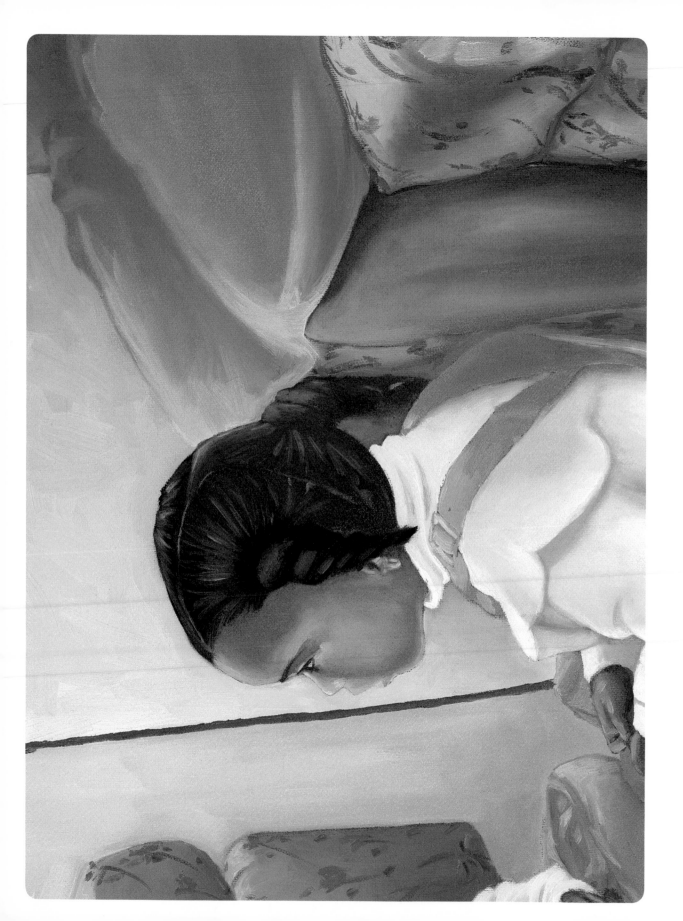

I try to do like Kyla in front of the mirror.
Kyla says, "Beautiful!"
I do like Kyla and say, "Beautiful!"

Oatmeal and apples for breakfast, and I do like Kyla, pouring honey on everything.

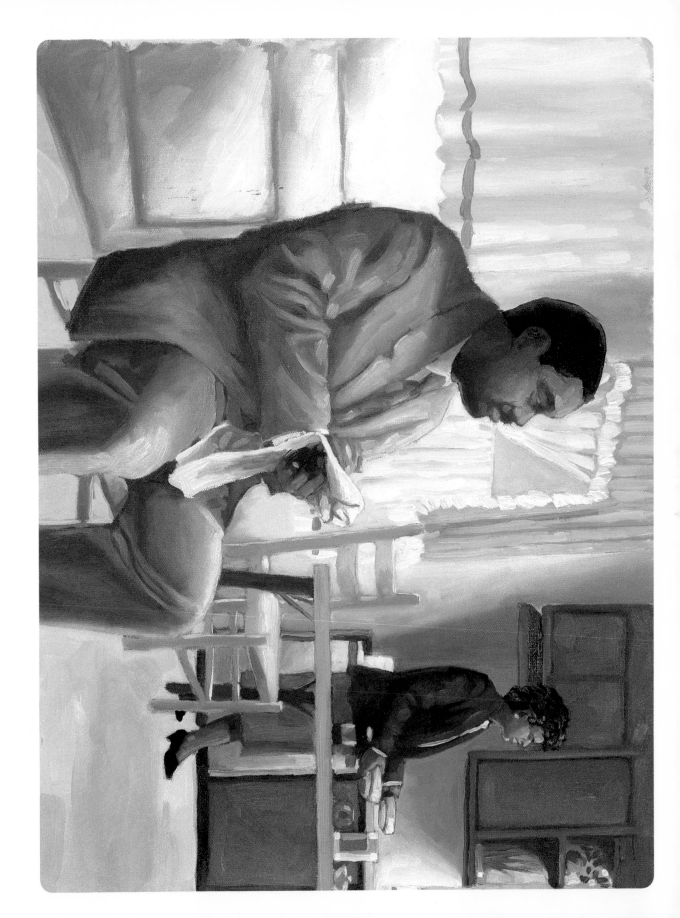

Mama says, "Lots of sunshine today."

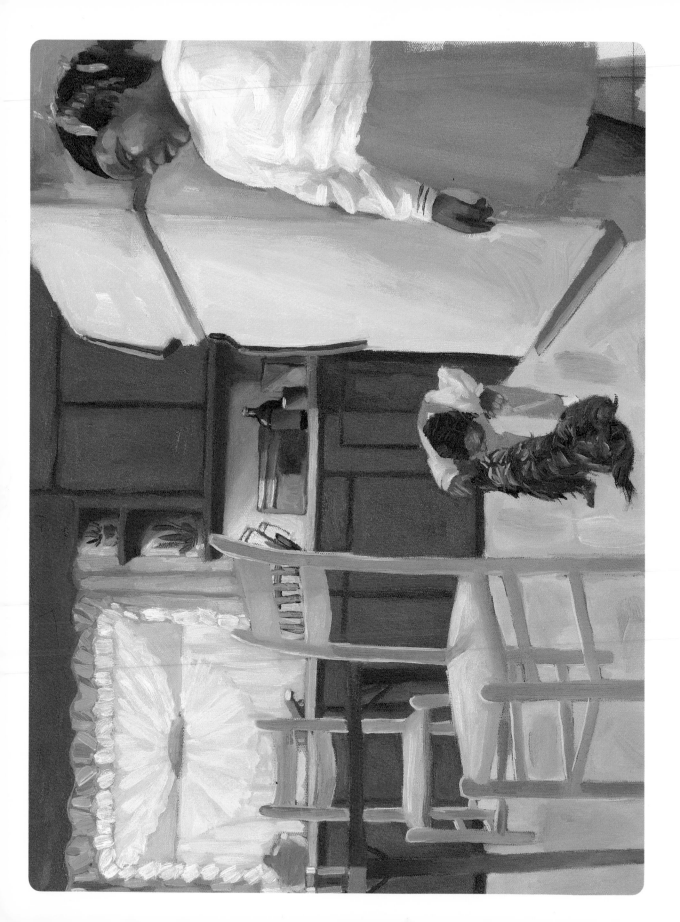

Kyla kisses the sunbeam on the dog's head.
I do like Kyla.

We're going to the store so Kyla helps me put my coat on.

"Warm now," she says.

I do like Kyla and say, "Warm now."

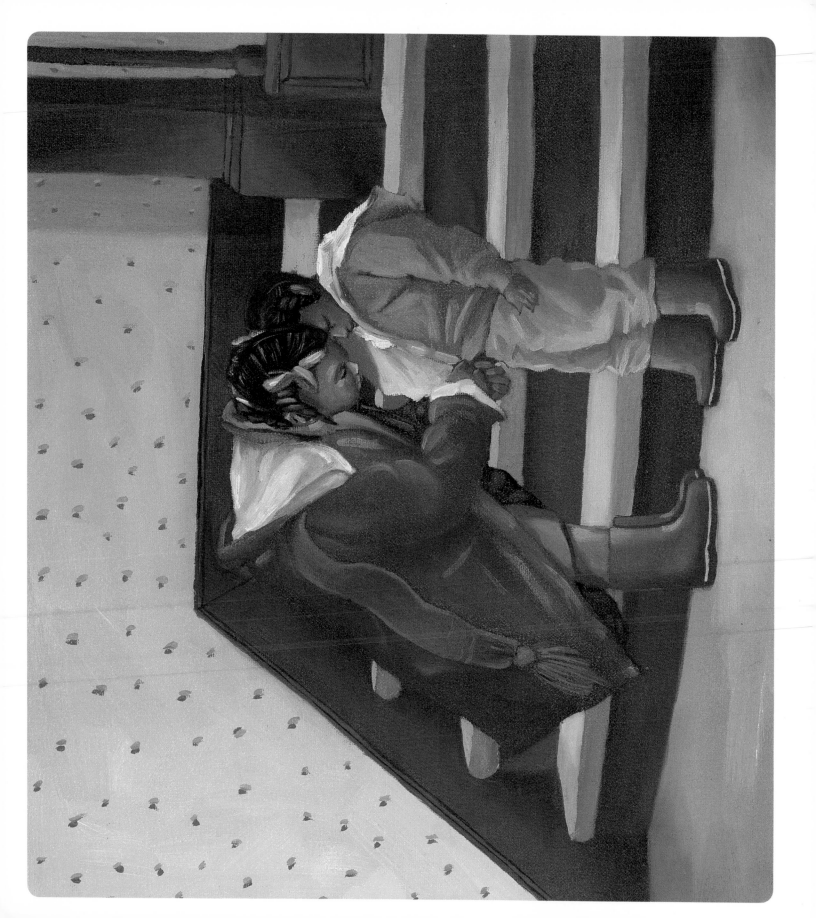

Got me some purple snow boots like Kyla, and we both crunch, crunch, crunch in the snow all the way to the store.

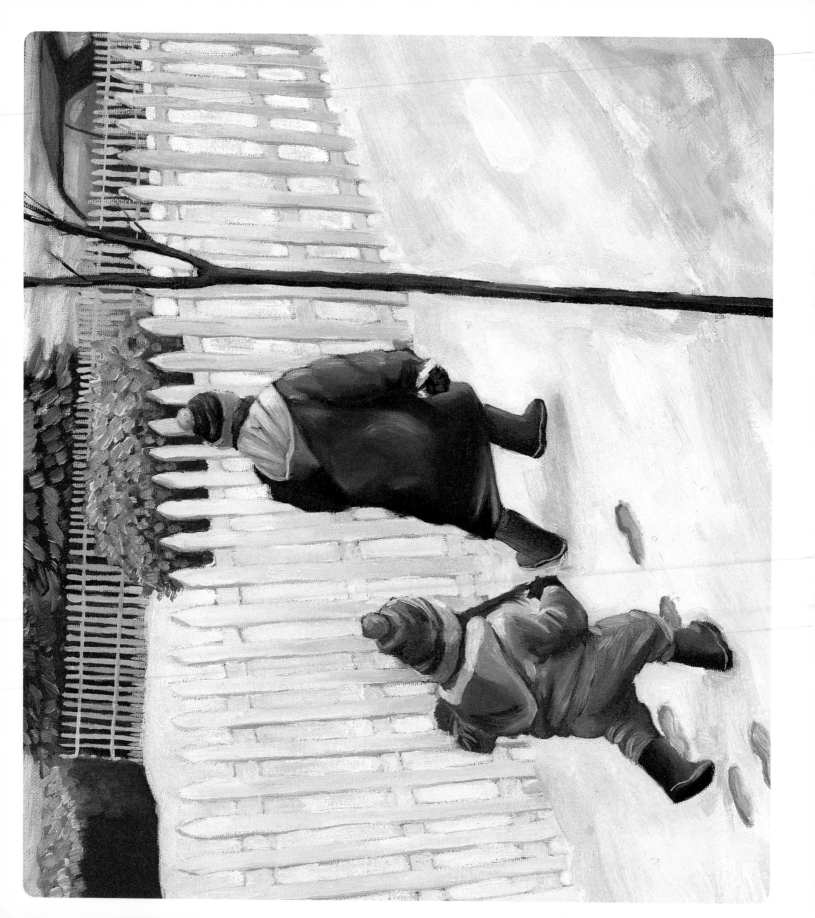

Past the big store window, I see myself.
I do like Kyla and skip past the window, watching....

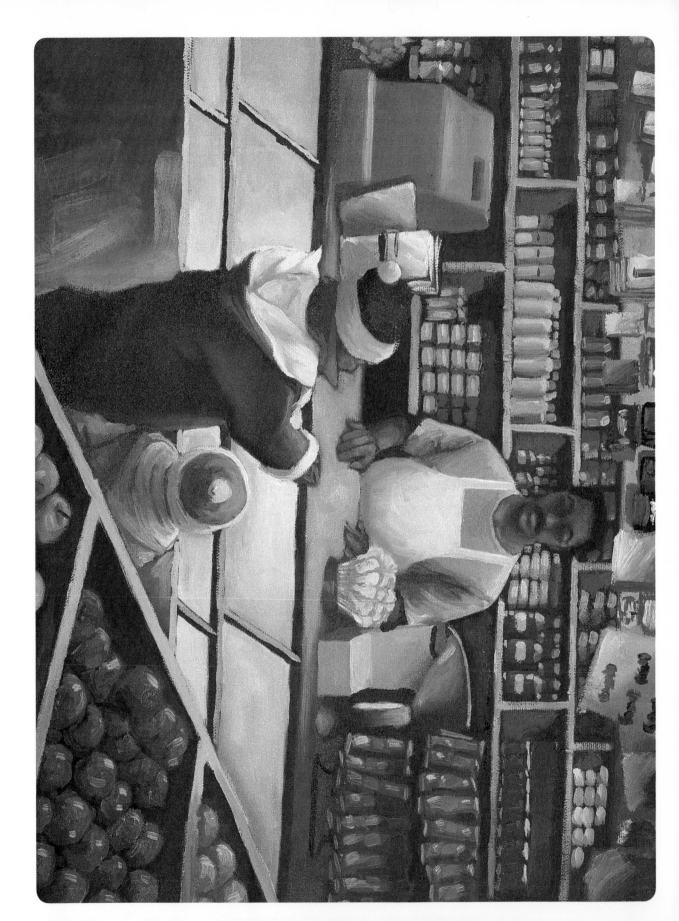

In the good-smelling store Kyla asks for cheese,
a bag of apples, and a jar of jam.

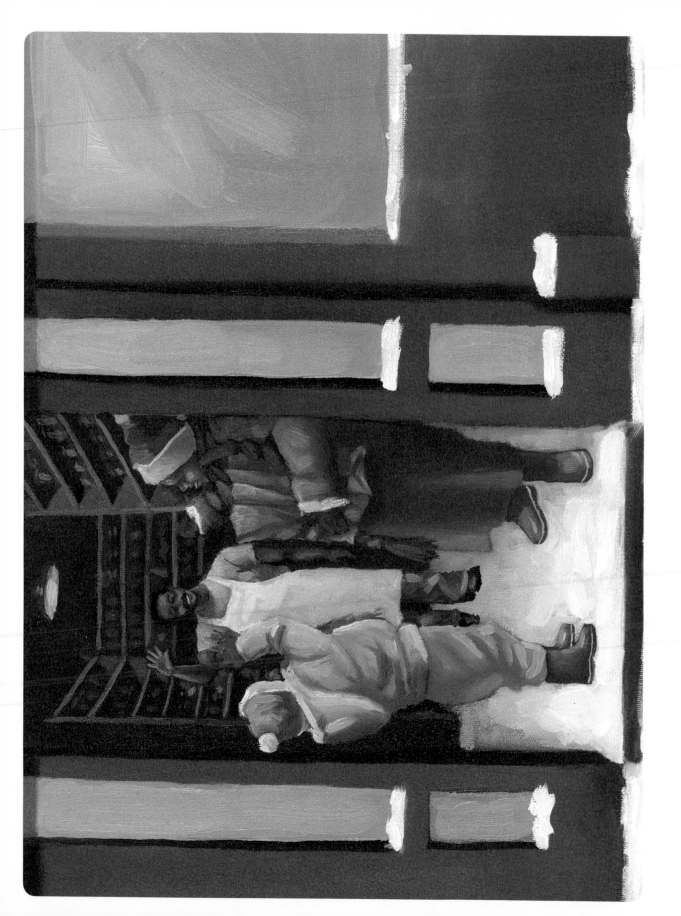

The man in the white apron says, "Goodbye and be good."
I do like Kyla and say, "OK, I will."

Kyla says, "Want to follow our footsteps back home?"
I do, just like Kyla.

Step, step, step.

"Read me a book, Kyla."

Kyla reads to me under the kitchen table.

I do like her and say, "The end," after the last page.

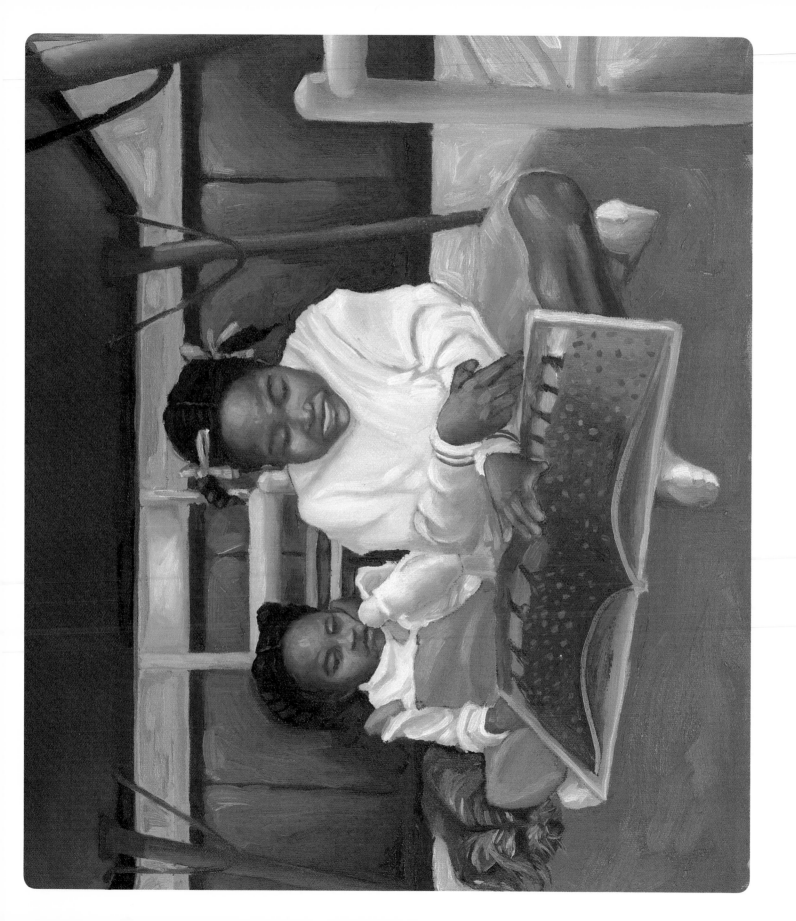

It's almost nighttime at the window.

Kyla says, "Birds must be asleep."

I tap at the window . . .

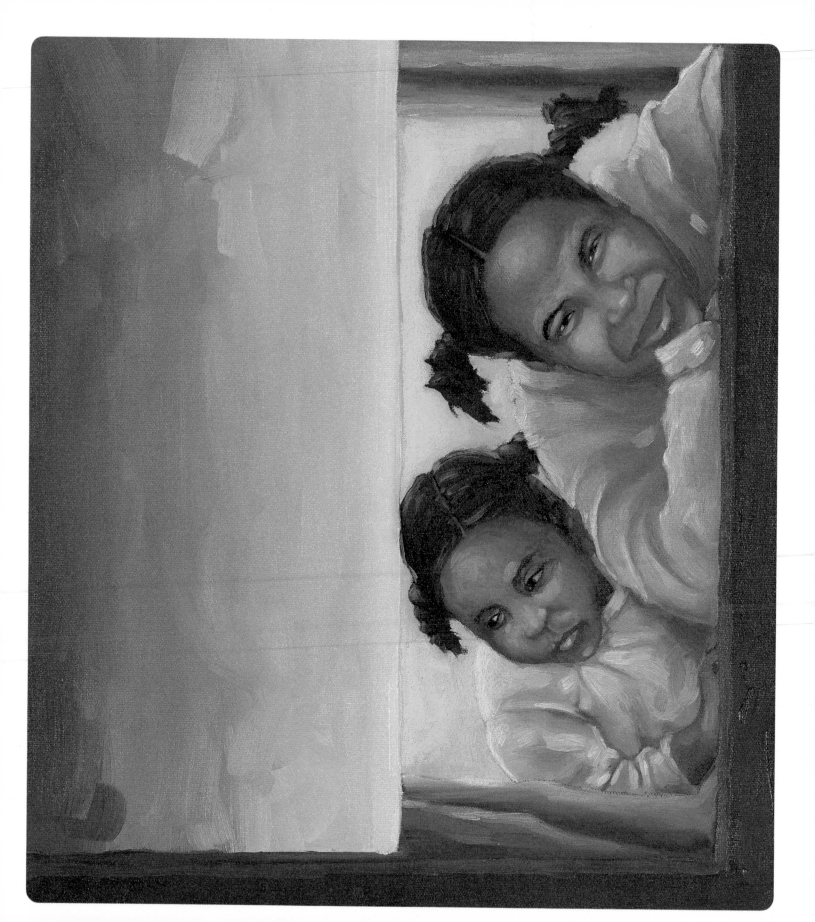

and Kyla does just like me.